EAST RIDING
OF YORKSHIRE COUNCIL
Schools Library Service

FICTION
2017

For Mary ~ J.D.

For Gill and Jessie, with love ~ A.C.

First published 2005 by Macmillan Children's Books
This edition published 2015 by Macmillan Children's Books
an imprint of Pan Macmillan,
20 New Wharf Road, London N1 9RR
Associated companies throughout the world
www.panmacmillan.com

ISBN: 978-1-4472-6612-9
Text copyright © Julia Donaldson 2005, 2015
Illustrations copyright © Anna Currey 2005, 2015
Moral rights asserted.

3 5 7 9 8 6 4 2

A CIP catalogue record for this book is available from the British Library

Printed in China

ROSIE'S
HAT

Written by Julia Donaldson

Illustrated by Anna Currey

Macmillan Children's Books

The wind blows high, the wind blows low.
PUFF, PUFF! BLOW, BLOW!

Rosie's hat blows off a cliff.

BOO-HOO! SNIFF, SNIFF!

A feather flutters on the breeze.
TICKLE, TICKLE! SNEEZE, SNEEZE!

The dog wakes up and sees the hat.
WOOF, WOOF! WHAT'S THAT?

Dog grabs hat and makes a dash.

SCAMPER, SCAMPER! SPLASH, SPLASH!

A fisherman has caught the hat.
BOTHER, BOTHER! DRAT, DRAT!

A screech owl flies above the beach.

FLAP, FLAP! SCREECH, SCREECH!

A mouse escapes an open beak.
PATTER, PATTER! SQUEAK, SQUEAK!

Some boys build castles with the hat.
SCOOP, SCOOP! PAT, PAT!

The hat is tossed into a tree.
ONE, TWO, THREE, WHEE!

Years go by, and little Rose

GROWS . . .

GROWS . . .

GROWS . . .

and GROWS.

Baby birds like worms to eat.
TWITTER, TWITTER! TWEET, TWEET!

The babies grow as weeks go by.
FLUTTER, FLUTTER! FLY, FLY!

Watch out, bird – here comes a cat.
WRIGGLE, POUNCE! HOWZAT?

Dog meets cat – whatever now?
WOOF, WOOF! MIAOW, MIAOW!

Stuck in a tree? You poor old thing!
BLEEP, BLEEP . . .

The rescue lady comes . . . it's Rose!
UP, UP! HERE GOES!

She's at the top! She's got the cat!

Well, well, fancy that . . .

FANCY THAT! IT'S ROSIE'S HAT!